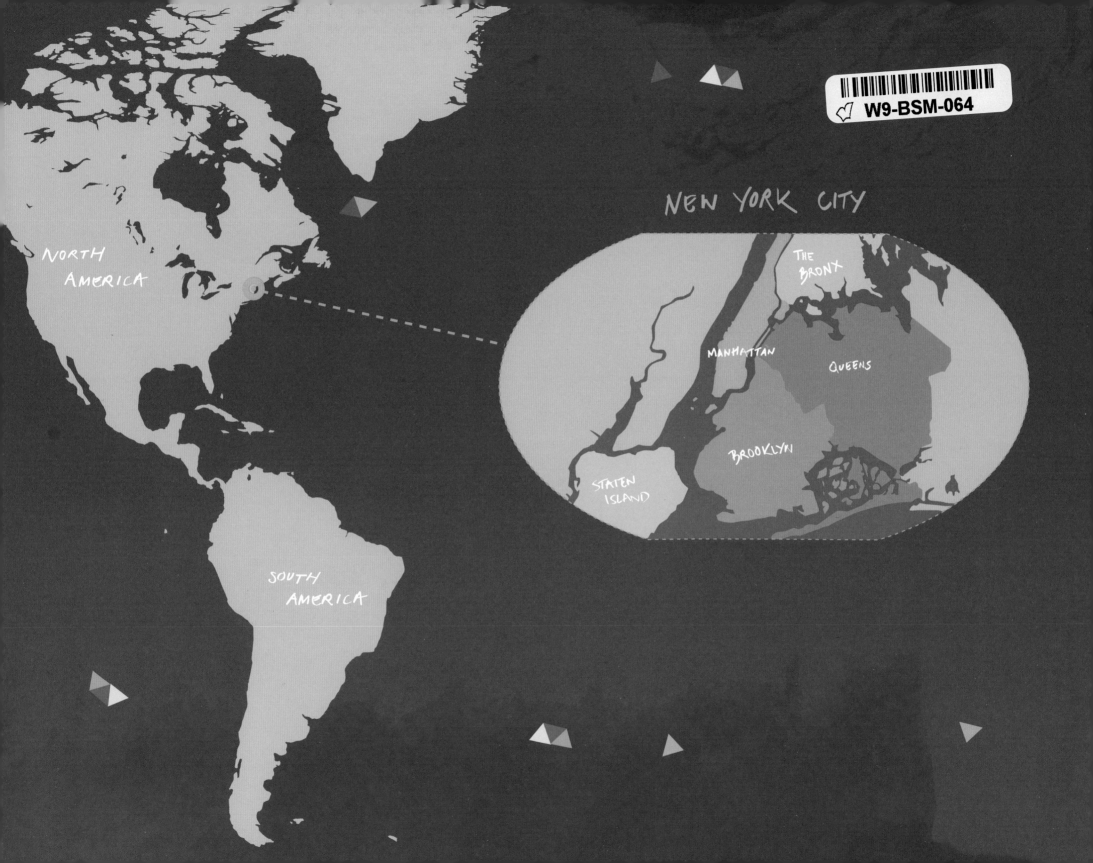

NORTH
AMERICA

SOUTH
AMERICA

NEW YORK CITY

THE
BRONX

MANHATTAN

QUEENS

BROOKLYN

STATEN
ISLAND

Published by Goff Books. An Imprint of ORO Editions
Gordon Goff: Publisher
www.goffbooks.com
info@goffbooks.com

10 9 8 7 6 5 4 3 2 1 First Edition

Library of Congress data available upon request.
World Rights: Available

ISBN: 978-1-940743-28-8

Color Separations and Printing: ORO Group Ltd.
Printed in China.
International Distribution: www.goffbooks.com/distribution

Designed by Sally Roydhouse Design
www.sallyroydhouse.com
www.findandseekbooks.com

FIND AND SEEK

NEW YORK

A Family's Guide to the City

Written and Illustrated by **SALLY ROYDHOUSE**

goff BOOKS

Down **U**nder **the M**anhattan **B**ridge **O**verpass, I run with my brother along the green grass.

Tall rectangles form the skyline
Stretching far along the horizon.
A compact city built on rock
Rises from the harbor block by block.

Over the river, a steel bridge suspends
Between solid stone book-ends.
The journey from Brooklyn to Manhattan
Is our first adventure's call to action.

BOROUGH HALL

You can walk across or catch a ferry,
My younger brother thinks that's too scary,
So our choice of the best thing to do
– Is to take the train, which tunnels through.

Standing in the narrow aisle,
Quick, put your ticket in the turnstile.
The clicking noise gives us a fright,
So we hold Dad's hand very tight.

Grab your metro card and map.
Give the platform buskers a clap.
Stay to the left, try to keep up,
Make way for others as you line up.

a dum, ta dum, the train wheels spin. Is the carriage too crowded for us to squeeze in? The doors slide open. "There's room for me." Choose a window seat so that you can **see**...

We are off on our subway journey. It's the easiest way to get around.
Watch the stations fly by as we head to midtown.

Mom and Dad have made a plan, and I'm ready to explore whatever we can.
What's in store for our day of fun? Our travelling challenge has just begun.

We arrive at Grand Central Station for a quick stop and take in the wonder of the rooftop, Constellations of stars stretch atop an arched blue ceiling backdrop.

Buy your tickets, keep on moving,
Lots of people busy commuting.
Tick-tock, **look** at the clock,
Hurry along, no time to stop.

hen stepping out onto 5th Avenue
You find an impressive street to wander through:
Steam from the subway escapes from below,
See the cabs and buses in bright yellow,
Smell the food truck vendors on the corner,
We're so hungry, let's place an order.

It's a fun part of travel, to try different foods. Its a way to learn what the local diet includes.

Pretzels, donuts, burgers and fries, *Cheesecake, pastrami, black beans and rice,* *Hot dogs, and pickles in bowls,* *Soft serve, and lobster rolls.*

Cupcakes deserve a mention of their own, there are many more flavors than at home...

Red velvet, peanut butter fudge

Oozy chocolate frosting smudge

Salted caramel lava spills

Lavender tea cake, toffee quills

Raspberry ganache nice and thick

...So many choices, it's hard to pick!

To find your bearings when you travel, head up to **watch** the view unravel.
Rockefeller's "Top of the Rock" is a tip for families who want to give the line a skip.

Upon the deck is 360 degrees of sprawling city as far as the eye can **see**.
Included is the Empire State building seen through telescopes for easy viewing.

An old rail track woven through the city
Is reclaimed as "The High Line" and it's a beauty.
Across 20 city blocks is a half-mile track,
Where families can enjoy a walk up and back.

You can follow along the walkway, and take part in activities of the day,
Or meander along amongst the flowers, **see** the sculptures, warehouses, and water towers.

THE ASTOR LIBRARY
FOUNDED BY
JOHN JACOB ASTOR
FOR THE
ADVANCEMENT OF USEFUL KNOWLEDGE
MDCCCXLVIII

THE LENOX LIBRARY
FOUNDED BY
JAMES LENOX
DEDICATED TO HISTORY
LITERATURE AND THE FINE ARTS
MDCCCLXX

THE TILDEN TRUST
FOUNDED BY
SAMUEL JONES TILDEN
TO SERVE THE INTERESTS OF
SCIENCE AND POPULAR EDUCATION
MDCCCLXXXV

MDCCCXCV ◎ THE NEW YORK PUBLIC LIBRARY ◎ MDCCCCII

The New York Public Library is a must to include in your diary.
And alongside this famous landmark, you will discover grassy Bryant Park.

Visit the carousel and outdoor reading room,
Borrow a book, but make sure to return it soon.
There is a little nook for kids to rest,
And a chance for parents to catch their breath.

The *Intrepid* is a humungous warship,
An aircraft carrier with a landing strip.
Boarding this boat is a little kid's dream,
A great place to explore and let off steam.

Climb high onto the flight deck,
Read the name of a fighter jet,
Or imagine you are in a rocket ship,
And learn a space shuttle survival tip.

For another day of discovery visit the Museum of Natural History,
Follow your nose or make a plan, explore every organism known to man.

Gorillas, lions, huge elephants, and Native Americans living in tents.
See birds of paradise in a tree, there is something here for everybody.

Take the Dino tour, it's full of wonders.
See skeletons of the great hunters.
In the hall of ocean life are sea monsters,
Where a gigantic whale from the ceiling hovers.

Dolphins, jellyfish, sea lions, and squid,
It's an amazing place for every kid!

Our favorite place to be,
With all there is to **see**,
Is Central Park of course.
It's a wonderland of sorts.

Starting at the North Woods, pretend you are Robin Hood. Scoot past the ravine towards the Loch,

There you can climb the huge flat rocks.

Belverdere Castle looms out of the green. Can you **see** a knight rescuing a queen?

Dodge the many dogs on a lead. Fly down the hill picking up speed!

At the Metropolitan Museum of Art,
Known as the MET for a start.
Be prepared with a map and guide,
To navigate the amazing things inside.

Ancient Egyptian mummies still intact,
Greek, Roman, and Asian artifacts,
Men in shining armor on horses,
Carrying spears that are enormous.

Catching a ferry is a great activity,
Which includes passing the Statue of Liberty.
Tugboats, helicopters, speed boats too,
There is a lot to **see** from the railing view.

Lady Liberty is a symbol of freedom,
A statue that shines on her city like a beacon.
With a crown and a blazing torch in her hand,
Her spirit is celebrated across the land.

Park Avenue is a grid of lights,
Taxi cabs and city brights.
Luckily Mom and Dad let us peek,
When we really should be asleep.

Our visit to New York has been such a treat,
It's a town with an energy that's hard to beat.
We have **seen** art, history, and tried amazing food,
But mostly it's been fun to **see** what New Yorkers do.

All kinds of people and places to **see**,
New York is an amazing place to be.

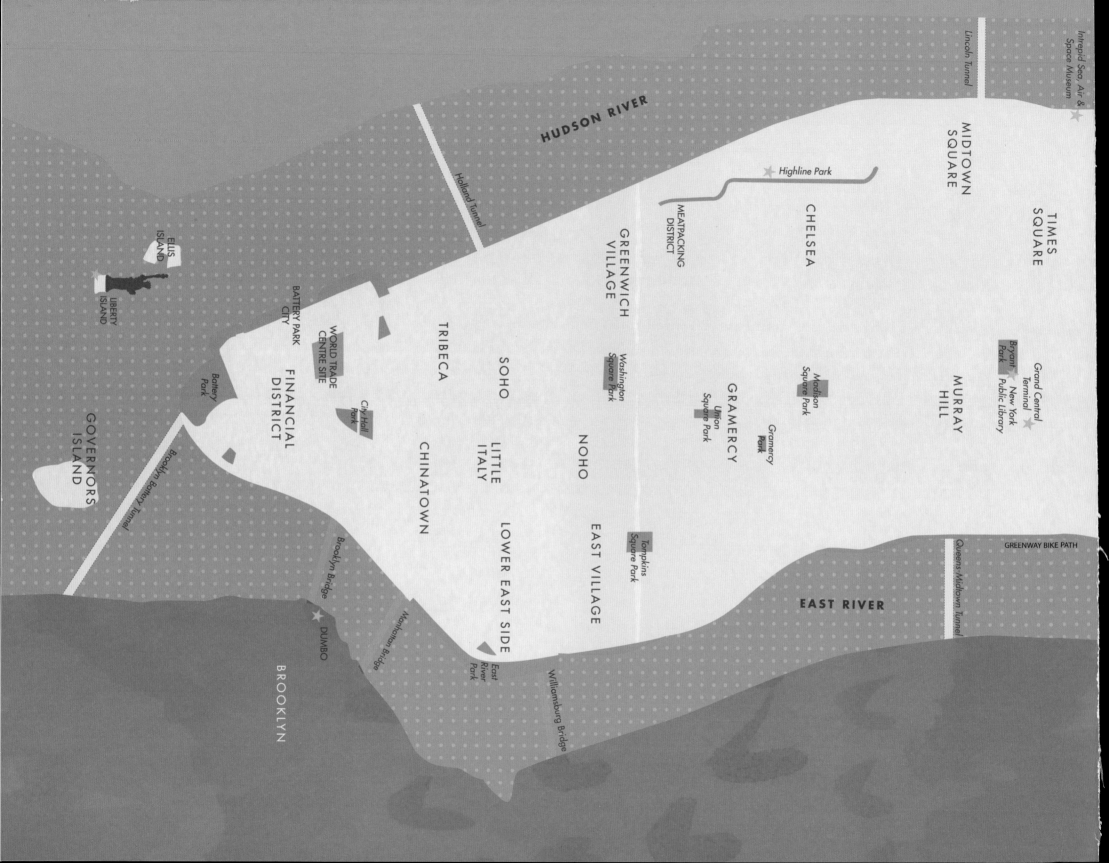

RECYCLING
AND UPCYCLING

SCIENCE • TECHNOLOGY • ENGINEERING

BY STEVEN OTFINOSKI

CHILDREN'S PRESS®

An Imprint of Scholastic Inc.

CONTENT CONSULTANT
Sherill Baldwin, Environmental Analyst, Connecticut Department of Energy and Environmental Protection

PHOTOGRAPHS ©: cover: Britt Erlanson/Getty Images; 3: Dave and Les Jacobs/Media Bakery; 4 left: The Granger Collection; 4 right: Mike Harrington/Getty Images; 5 left: Monty Rakusen/Media Bakery; 5 right: Media Bakery; 6: Steve Marcus/AP Images; 8: Art Media/The Image Works; 9: Jacob A. Riis/Getty Images; 10 left: F. Gutekunst/Library of Congress; 10 right-11 left, 11 right: The Granger Collection; 12: war posters/Alamy Images; 13: Marty Lederhandler/AP Images; 14 left: Universal History Archive/Getty Images; 14 right-15 bottom: The Keasbury-Gordon Photograph Archive/Alamy Images; 15 top: Joerg Boethling/Alamy Images; 16: Eric Taylor/ Getty Images; 17: Andrew Link/AP Images; 18: Mike Harrington/Getty Images; 20: PathDoc/Shutterstock, Inc.; 21: Prisma/Superstock, Inc.; 22 left: Dave and Les Jacobs/Media Bakery; 22 right-23 left: David Leahy/Media Bakery; 23 right: Jim West/Superstock, Inc.; 24: Richard Levine/Alamy Images; 25: Ariel Skelley/Media Bakery; 26 top: Raymond Boyd/Getty Images; 26 bottom: Edwin Remsberg/Alamy Images; 27: Amy Davis/Getty Images; 28: rfletcher/Alamy Images; 29: Brian Vander Brug/Getty Images; 30: imageBROKER/Superstock, Inc.; 32: Hero Images/Media Bakery; 33: Diane Collins/Jordan Hollender/Media Bakery; 34: Kim Karpeles/Alamy Images; 35: Richard B. Levine/Newscom; 38: Monty Rakusen/Media Bakery; 39: Dan Bannister/Media Bakery; 40 left: CB2/ZOB/Newscom; 40 right-41 left: Oli Scarff/Getty Images; 41 right: Steven Siewert/Getty Images; 42: wavebreakmedia/Shutterstock, Inc.; 43: Don Mason/Media Bakery; 44: Media Bakery; 46: Jupiterimages/ Media Bakery; 47: Richard B. Levine/Newscom; 48 top: Robert Galbraith/Landov; 48 bottom, 48 top: Justin Sullivan/Getty Images; 48 bottom: Aurora Photos/Alamy Images; 50: David Leahy/Media Bakery; 51: Lourens Smak/Alamy Images; 52 left: Media Bakery; 52 right: B Christopher/Alamy Images; 53: Hero Images/Media Bakery; 54: Monty Rakusen/Media Bakery; 55: Coprid/Shutterstock, Inc.; 56: Rafael Campillo/Superstock, Inc.; 57: Dragan Zivkovic/Alamy Images; 58: PEAT International, Inc./AP Images; 59: Eric Risberg/AP Images.

LIBRARY OF CONGRESS CATALOGING-IN-PUBLICATION DATA
Otfinoski, Steven, author.
 Recycling and upcycling : science, technology, and engineering / by Steven Otfinoski.
  pages cm. — (Calling all innovators: a career for you)
  ISBN 978-0-531-23002-2 (library binding) — ISBN 978-0-531-23220-0 (pbk.)
 1. Environmental sciences—Vocational guidance—Juvenile literature. 2. Recycling (Waste, etc.)—
Vocational guidance—Juvenile literature. 3. Salvage (Waste, etc.)—Juvenile literature.
 4. Environmentalists—Juvenile literature. I. Title. II. Series: Calling all innovators.
  GE60.O84 2015
  363.72'82—dc23   2015029119

All rights reserved. Published in 2016 by Children's Press, an imprint of Scholastic Inc.
Printed in the United States of America 113

1 2 3 4 5 6 7 8 9 10 R 25 24 23 22 21 20 19 18 17 16

Science, technology, engineering, the arts, and math are the fields that drive innovation. Whether they are finding ways to make our lives easier or developing the latest entertainment, the people who work in these fields are changing the world for the better. Do you have what it takes to join the ranks of today's greatest innovators? Read on to discover if a career in the exciting world of recycling and upcycling is for you.

TABLE *of* CONTENTS

A street sweeper helps clean up New York City in the late 1800s.

Composting is a great way to reuse food scraps and yard waste.

Skilled workers are required to watch over the recycling process.

Plastic bottles are among the many everyday items that can be recycled.

At Apex and other landfills, loaders and bulldozers are used to compact trash. Good compaction reduces odors and rodents.

1

CYCLES THROUGH TIME

The largest landfill in the United States lies in a valley just 20 miles (32 kilometers) north of Las Vegas, Nevada. The Apex Landfill contains 59 million tons of trash. This mountain of garbage covers 300 acres (121 hectares) and reaches a peak height of 300 feet (91.4 meters). Opened in 1993, Apex is expected to be used for 250 years. By that time, it will cover more than 2,200 acres (890 ha).

Compared to most of the landfills in America, Apex is well designed and environmentally friendly. An underground plastic lining prevents garbage from polluting the water table and surrounding soil. However, Apex is also a grim reminder of the growing problem of waste management around the world. As landfills fill up, where will we put our trash? How will we stop poisoning our water, land, and air with the things we throw away? The answers to these questions can be summed up in one word—recycling.

LANDMARK LANDFILLS

400 BCE	1937 CE	1974	1993
The world's first **municipal** landfill is established in Athens, Greece.	The Fresno Municipal Sanitary Landfill, the first modern U.S. landfill, opens in California.	Mount Trashmore Park in Virginia Beach, Virginia, opens on the site of an abandoned landfill.	Apex Landfill is established outside Las Vegas, Nevada.

THE EARLY DAYS

People have found ways to conserve and reuse their resources since ancient times. Archaeologists have found recycled glass products in ancient cities such as Sagalassos in what is now Turkey. The ancient Romans melted statues to create new statues or bronze coins. In the Middle Ages, people in Great Britain used ashes from fires as an ingredient in bricks.

"Rag-and-bone men" in the 1800s collected rags, animal bones, and metal products from homes and sold them to small businesses. These businesses used the rags to make papers and ground up the bones for fertilizer. Farmers collected garbage from restaurants to feed their livestock. They used the animals' manure as fertilizer for crops.

A rag-and-bone man walks the streets of Paris, France, in the late 1800s.

BASKET FOR CARRYING RECYCLABLE MATERIALS

In New York City and other large cities, garbage began to pile up in the streets during the 1800s.

THE INDUSTRIAL REVOLUTION

Throughout much of history, manufactured goods in Europe and America were mostly made by hand. This made them expensive. People got the most of their purchases by finding ways to **upcycle** goods for other purposes or recycle them into new products.

This all changed with the Industrial Revolution in the early 1800s. Newly invented machines could turn out products faster and more cheaply than craftspeople working by hand. People bought these goods at a fraction of their former prices. They could afford to dispose of worn-out things and buy new ones. All this garbage soon began piling up. In earlier times, people would bury their own waste. Now, land had to be set aside for **dumps**. Even then, most garbage was tossed into the streets, especially in cities. It mixed with animal and human waste and water. It was unsightly, it smelled bad, and it spread germs and disease. Something had to be done.

George Waring, Jr., knew that cleaner cities would help prevent deadly illnesses.

FROM MEMPHIS TO NEW YORK

Waring had already had a long career as an engineer and designer of sanitation systems. In 1878, he had created a successful sewer system for Memphis, Tennessee. This helped end a series of yellow fever and cholera **epidemics** that were spread, in part, through the filthy water. In New York, Waring set up a unit of street sweepers who dressed in uniforms and were called the White Wings.

AMERICA'S FIRST RECYCLING CENTER

Until 1895, New York City, like other American cities, had no organized program for waste management or recycling. That year Colonel George Waring, Jr., a Civil War veteran, was appointed the city's **Sanitation** Commissioner.

THE APOSTLE OF CLEANLINESS

Waring's plan required New York residents to separate their garbage into bins by type: food waste, ashes from stoves, paper, and street sweepings. In 1897, he set up a recycling center in Manhattan with "picking yards." Here workers would pick through the trash and pull out paper, metal containers, and other things that could be recycled and made into new products. It

A member of the White Wings poses with his broom in 1896.

CART FOR COLLECTING WASTE

WHITE UNIFORM

Street cleaners similar to the White Wings continued working in New York City for many decades.

was the beginning of modern recycling. Waring's efforts in sanitation earned him the title Apostle of Cleanliness.

A TRAGIC END

Waring left New York in 1898 to study waste removal in Cuba. He hoped to bring the success he had in Memphis and New York to yet another location. However, Waring contracted yellow fever, a disease he had helped conquer in Memphis. He died at age 65. ✳

A Gas Mask requires 1.11 pounds of rubber

A Life Raft requires 17 to 100 pounds of rubber

A Scout Car requires 306 pounds of rubber

A Heavy Bomber requires 1,825 pounds of rubber

America needs your
SCRAP RUBBER

Posters helped encourage citizens to donate recyclable materials to the war effort during World War II.

A NEED FOR RECYCLING

A serious movement to conserve, reuse, and recycle resources took place during the Great Depression in the 1930s, when millions of people around the world were out of work and had little money. They couldn't afford to buy new things and had to find ways to reuse what they had. They repaired their worn-out products and found creative ways to upcycle items into new uses, such as making clothes from flour sacks.

When the United States entered World War II in 1941, recycling and upcycling became a patriotic duty. The government **rationed** things such as metal and rubber because they were important resources for the military. Many food items were also rationed. In response, people planted "victory gardens" in their yards, growing their own vegetables and fruits. They also used food scraps to create **compost**.

RECYCLING LOST AND FOUND

When the war ended in 1945, America experienced an economic boom. The average person could now afford new products such as cars, stereo systems, and television sets. The country forgot the benefits of recycling as people kept buying new things. Land was cheap, and it was easier for people to toss all their discarded things into municipal dumps and landfills than to recycle.

The 1960s saw great change in these attitudes. People turned their attention to preserving the environment from pollution. By the 1970s, people were rediscovering the importance of recycling as a part of a growing **conservation** movement. By the 1980s, curbside collection of such recyclables as newspapers, metal cans, glass jars, and plastic bottles was becoming a regular part of life across America.

Protecting the environment became a major issue for many people during the 1960s and 1970s.

GARY ANDERSON

The recycling logo that appears on millions of recycling bins and other products was created in 1970 by a 23-year-old student at the University of Southern California. Gary Anderson submitted his design to a competition for a recycling symbol run by the Container Corporation of America. It won out over 500 other entries. Anderson's design was simple and direct. It showed three folded arrows in a continuous cycle, one pointing to the next. The three arrows are meant to represent the three main steps of recycling: the collection of recyclables, the manufacture of new products from them, and the purchase and use of these products. Over the years, Anderson's design has become one of the most recognized logos in the world. It is used to promote recycling everywhere.

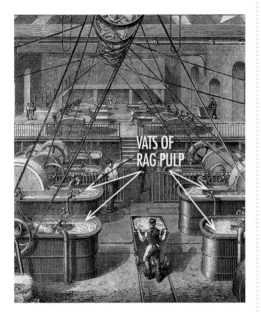

VATS OF
RAG PULP

Old rags were bleached and mixed with water to make pulp for paper.

A REVOLUTION IN PAPERMAKING

Newspaper is one of the most recycled materials today. However, paper was once a scarce resource that was commonly made from rags and old clothing. In 1690, at paper mills like the one near Philadelphia (the first to open in America), discarded clothing and rags were beaten into **pulp** and then poured into molds to make paper. But by the 1850s, rags were in short supply, and there was an increasing demand for daily newspapers.

FROM RAGS TO WOOD

Inventors began seeking new ways of making paper. Eventually, they discovered that wood pulp from trees could be transformed into paper with the help of chemicals. In 1868, the first wood pulp sawmill opened in Topsham, Maine. It produced one ton of wood pulp per day. This pulp could be turned into paper cheaply and quickly.

Printers needed plenty of paper to meet the demand for newspapers.

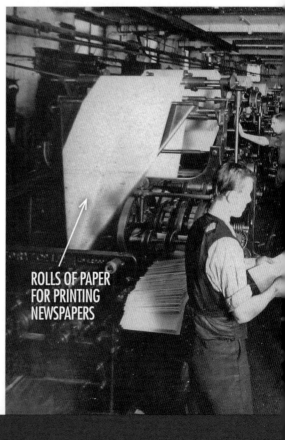

ROLLS OF PAPER
FOR PRINTING
NEWSPAPERS

Piles of wood chips are set aside to be turned into pulp at a mill in Uruguay. Recycling reduces the amount of natural resources used to make new paper and other products.

THE PAPER PROCESS

By the 1930s, almost all paper in the United States was made from wood pulp instead of rags. But while this made paper production easier, it also led to more trees being cut down to make pulp. As people work to conserve trees and other natural resources today, they search for more and more effective ways to turn used paper and cardboard back into pulp. ☀

GOGGLES, MASKS, AND
EARMUFFS PROTECT WORKERS
FROM NOISE AND INJURY

CONVEYOR BELTS
MOVE RECYCLABLE
MATERIALS
THROUGH THE MRF

Workers sort through recyclables at a Materials Recovery Facility.

RECYCLING PAPER AND PLASTIC

From curbside pickup, loose paper, junk mail, and newspapers are taken to either a **transfer station** or Materials Recovery Facility (MRF). They are then bundled to be sold to paper mills. At the mills, the paper is chopped up into tiny pieces and soaked in water and chemicals to be returned to the pulp from which it came. Chemicals remove ink from the paper, and wood fiber is added to strengthen the recycled pulp. The recycled paper is then sold to manufacturers to be made once more into products such as newspapers, books, and cardboard boxes. It is also used in paper products such as paper towels and toilet paper.

Used plastic bottles and jars are collected and delivered to facilities where they are also shredded into tiny pieces. The pieces are heated and treated with chemicals. This transforms them into a thick, sticky liquid. The liquid plastic is then used to create useful products, such as outdoor furniture and carpets.

GLASS AND METAL

Early soda manufacturers had a good way to recycle their product. With the deposit refund system, customers were charged a small deposit of 5 or 10 cents for each bottle purchased. The deposit was fully refunded when the empty glass bottles were returned to the stores. The bottles could then be washed and reused. Today, most large beverage manufacturers have stopped washing the old bottles and reusing them. Instead, the glass is crushed, melted, and formed into new products as part of the recycling process. Some smaller businesses still use refillable bottles because they are so environmentally friendly. But in general, glass bottles have been replaced by plastic bottles.

Since the 1950s, steel and aluminum cans have become popular. Like plastic or glass bottles, they are recyclable. The cans are shredded into pieces and then melted down in a furnace at high temperatures. The liquid metal is cooled and then hardened into blocks. The blocks are pressed flat by machines into thin sheets. These sheets can be shaped into new cans. Aluminum is the most valuable of all recycled materials. In spite of this, Americans throw away about $1 billion worth of aluminum cans each year instead of recycling them.

Bottles must be washed carefully if they are to be filled again.

Composting is a great way to recycle food scraps, yard waste, and other materials instead of throwing them away.

2

A WORLD OF RECYCLING

I t's a lovely summer morning in the Hernandez household. After breakfast, Mrs. Hernandez puts the coffee grounds and food scraps in a compost pile in the backyard. This material will later be used to enrich the soil in the family's garden. Her son, Juan, starts his daily chores. This includes vacuuming the new living room carpet that is made entirely of recycled plastic. Amazingly, it looks and feels like any other carpet.

Mr. and Mrs. Hernandez gather up their cloth bags to go food shopping. The bags conserve resources because they are reusable. They won't pollute the environment like the store's plastic bags. Daughter Marie goes outside with her novel, printed on recycled paper, and sits down to read on a lounge chair that is also made entirely of recycled plastic.

Recycling and using recycled products have become a big part of life in the 21st century. The more we recycle, the less waste we throw away that could harm the environment. The great strides we've taken in recycling are making our world a better place to live.

HIGHLIGHTS IN RECYCLING

1897	1968	1973	1976
The first U.S. recycling center is established in New York City.	Aluminum companies begin recycling discarded aluminum cans and other products.	The nation's first curbside recycling program begins in Berkeley, California.	The U.S. government passes the Resource Conservation and Recovery Act to help conserve resources and reduce waste.

FROM COLORED PAPER TO COFFEE CUPS

One-fourth of all garbage is paper, and almost all of this paper is recyclable. Until recently, some kinds of paper products were not recyclable, but new technology is changing that. For example, colored paper once could not be mixed with white paper. Now some paper mills are using a new process to remove colored ink. Once the paper has been shredded and made into pulp, air bubbles are injected into it. The ink sticks to the bubbles and rises to the paper's surface, where it can be skimmed off.

Disposable coffee cups have long been banned from recycling centers due a plastic coating that keeps liquid from seeping out of them. In the United Kingdom alone, 2.5 billion of these cups have ended up in landfills each year. Now a British company has developed a process that makes them recyclable. The cup is softened in a warm liquid solution. Then the plastic coating is separated from the paper fiber and skimmed off. The high-grade pulp that remains is remade into quality paper products.

Finding ways to recycle common items such as paper coffee cups can dramatically cut down the amount of trash we produce.

Glass cullet can be made into new bottles or a variety of other products.

GLASS MADE NEW

Crushed glass from beverage bottles and food jars, called cullet, is often unusable for making new bottles and jars because it is **contaminated** with other materials. Some of it ends up as construction material or being used for covering landfills. But today at recycling centers and MRFs, new methods are allowing more glass to be recycled. Magnets pull out metal caps and lids from the stream of glass. Colored glass is then separated out from the more desirable clear glass. Air jets blow the clear glass onto another conveyor belt. The clear crushed glass is sold to bottle manufacturers to be made into new bottles and jars. Thanks to this improved technology, 90 percent of the bottle glass recycled today is used to make new bottles. Companies save millions of dollars by using recycled glass rather than making glass from raw materials.

MODERN MARVEL

Separating recyclables into different containers makes it easier for MRFs to sort and process them.

SINGLE-STREAM RECYCLING

Until about 15 years ago, people had to separate their curbside recyclables into two or more bins. Paper products went in one bin. Plastics, glass, and metal went in another. This is called dual-stream recycling. Recycling trucks had separate compartments into which workers would empty the different bins. But this began to change when single-stream recycling was introduced in the late 1990s. This method allows people to put all their recyclables into a single container. The recyclables are then brought to an MRF to be separated and sorted. Today, many towns and cities have single-stream recycling programs.

HIGH-TECH SEPARATING

At an MRF, new technology helps separate the recyclables so they can be sold to manufacturers and reused. Powerful magnets separate metal products from the single stream. Giant fans blow out paper products. Screens separate flat paper from round containers. Many of these facilities are partially or totally automated, which makes the process move very quickly.

A BETTER WAY

Single-stream recycling encourages more people to participate in recycling. It also makes it easier for workers to collect the recyclables. Finally, single-streaming encourages what experts call "three bin collection." With only one bin needed for recyclables, a second bin can be used for compostable food scraps and yard cuttings. The third bin is for trash. Because so much material goes into the other two bins, much less trash is produced.

In single-stream recycling, all types of recyclables are separated at the recycling facility.

After materials are separated, they are compacted into large bales.

MANY TYPES OF RECYCLABLES IN THE SAME STREAM

THE DOWNSIDE

While single-stream recycling has many advantages, there is still room to improve this process. Cross-contamination of glass, metal, and plastics can occur, which lowers the value of recyclables. Experts estimate that single-stream recycling costs $3.00 more per ton of recyclables than dual-stream recycling. However, as technology improves, this cross-contamination may be largely eliminated. ✺

Every year, millions of plastic bottles end up in landfills instead of recycling centers.

NEW PROCESSES FOR PLASTICS

Plastic is a popular material for making many products because it is so cheap and durable. However, not all plastics are the same. Some are easy to recycle. Others are not. Some are safe to use with food and drinks, while others can cause health problems.

Because there are so many different kinds of plastic recyclables, sorting them is critical. When done by hand, this process can be extremely time-consuming. However, scientists at Ludwig-Maximilian University in Munich, Germany, have found a way to speed things up. A flash of light beamed on each plastic item causes it to **fluoresce**, or glow. Special sensors measure how long it takes for the fluorescence to fade. Each plastic type fluoresces for a different amount of time. This allows the sensors to instantly identify and sort the different types of plastic.

THE PLASTIC BAG PROBLEM

Plastic shopping bags are a major source of waste in the world today. An estimated 100 billion of these flimsy containers are discarded in the United States alone each year. They choke landfills. They suffocate animals in the wild. They are eaten by fish and other sea life, killing them. They are also a tremendous waste of resources. It takes 11 barrels of oil to produce a ton of plastic bags.

Increasing use of easily recyclable paper bags and reusable cloth bags is beginning to solve the problem. Scientists are also developing plastic bags that **biodegrade** much faster than regular plastic bags. Oxo-biodegradable plastic is one of the best of these new inventions. Additives in the plastic cause it to break down when exposed to sunlight or heat. Bacteria and other microscopic creatures can then easily digest the plastic. Disposed bags could degrade completely within a year. The bags are also easy to recycle and make into other plastic products.

Reusable shopping bags help conserve natural resources by cutting down on the amount of plastic that people use.

MODERN MARVEL

SOLAR PANELS

WHEEL SPINS TO POWER CONVEYOR BELT THAT LIFTS TRASH FROM THE WATER

The Inner Harbor Water Wheel prevents trash from reaching the Atlantic Ocean.

A NEW KIND OF WATERWHEEL

The waterwheel is one of the wonders of early human technology. This device uses the power of running water to grind grain and other raw resources in mills. But in Baltimore, Maryland, a new use has been found for this historic machine: keeping trash out of the ocean. The Inner Harbor Water Wheel sits at the mouth of the Jones Falls River, where the river flows into the harbor and then the Atlantic Ocean. Rivers like the Jones Falls carry tons of trash, especially plastic bags, into the sea where they can harm fish and other sea

Trash catches on ridges in the wheel's conveyor belt and is lifted out of the water.

life. The bags and other garbage enter the waterway via storm drains from the ground and streets.

CATCHING THE TRASH

As the river flows, it causes the wheel to turn. When the water current isn't strong enough to turn the wheel, solar cells use the sun's energy to make it spin. Compartments in the wheel trap the trash, lift it out of the water, and deposit it into a barge that serves as a dumpster. When the barge is full, a boat tows it to a waste-to-energy plant. There, the trash is burned to provide electricity for nearby homes and businesses. A new, empty barge immediately replaces the full one. Every day, the Baltimore waterwheel removes as much as 50,000 pounds (22,678 kilograms) of trash from the river, or more than 9,000 tons each year. In the future, similar wheels could be used to help keep other waterways clean. ✺

Workers clear out the waterwheel after it became clogged with an excess of trash after a rainstorm in 2008.

METAL MAGIC

After plastics, metal is the biggest waste problem we face today. Aluminum cans are an especially major issue. It takes 500 years for one of these cans to biodegrade in a landfill. The good news is that more and more aluminum is being recycled. Making an aluminum can from recycled metal uses 90 percent less energy than making a new can from raw materials. In addition, aluminum can be recycled over and over again endlessly. However, different cans contain different **alloys**. They must be sorted before being recycled to avoid mixing them together.

Manual sorting is slow and costly. So scientists at the Palo Alto Research Center (PARC) in California have come up with a quicker way to identify alloys and sort metal. They have developed a substance that electrically "excites" each item, quickly identifying its alloys. Current x-ray fluorescence techniques take more than a minute to analyze the alloys in metal objects. The PARC equipment can do it in one-tenth of a second.

Aluminum cans are crushed and compacted into blocks that can be easily transported.

Workers load a truck with used electronics at a recycling event for residents of Los Angeles, California.

E-WASTE

Recycling bottles, cans, and newspapers is one thing. But what should people do with old computers, TV sets, and cell phones? Millions of Americans simply drop these items off at the local dump or landfill. This electronic waste, known as e-waste, is an ongoing challenge, and the problem is growing daily.

One answer is to donate your old electronics to people who could use them. Computers and cell phones often have a lot of life left in them, even after we replace them with newer models. Charities and schools can use them. There are also companies that send used electronic devices overseas to schools and communities in developing countries where they are desperately needed. If you can't donate, you should take your discarded electronics to a recycling center, where they can be either disassembled for recyclables and reusable parts or disposed of responsibly.

Recycling is becoming
more and more popular
as people realize its
many benefits.

ON THE JOB

A s the challenge of conserving resources, protecting the environment, and reducing waste becomes a primary concern for Americans, more people will be needed to work in this important industry. According to government statistics, around 1.1 million people are employed in the collecting, processing, manufacturing, and reusing of recyclable materials today. This number will continue to grow as communities fully commit to recycling. From the drivers who operate recycling trucks to the line workers at MRFs to the engineers and scientists who are working to improve recycling methods, many different workers are needed to keep the recycling stream flowing effectively.

LEGAL MILESTONES

1657	1899	1986	2007
New Amsterdam, which later became New York City, passes a law against residents throwing garbage into the streets.	Dumping garbage in navigable waterways is restricted under the federal Rivers and Harbors Act.	Rhode Island establishes the first statewide mandatory recycling law in the United States.	San Francisco becomes the first American city to ban the distribution of plastic bags in grocery stores.

Scientists collect water samples and test them in the lab to ensure that recycling facilities follow environmental regulations.

SCIENTISTS OF RECYCLING

No matter how effective they are, all waste management programs impact natural and human environments. It is the job of environmental scientists to study and measure that impact, report their findings, and work with government and businesses to lessen it.

Government agencies employ scientists to see that recycling and waste management companies are meeting regulations to protect human health and the environment. Environmental chemists and biologists analyze water and soil samples where waste is given off by recycling processes. They evaluate the impact of chemicals in the environment and design ways to reduce waste and clean up existing pollution. This helps keep the environment safe for plant, animal, and human life.

Other scientists study materials to find new ways of recycling them. This might mean creating new types of plastic that are more easily recycled, finding new ways to break materials down so they can be reused, and much more.

REUSING RARE EARTH METALS

Many products are made using valuable materials that are difficult to remove and reuse. For example, rare earth metals, used in computers, televisions, and other electronic products, are in short supply in many parts of the world. These materials are built into the products and intertwined with many other substances in a complex arrangement. Recycling them isn't as simple as putting them on a conveyor belt and letting a machine sort them. Scientists are always searching for new ways to harvest these materials so they don't go to waste. At a Belgian university, environmental chemists have developed a process for extracting two kinds of rare earth metals from fluorescent lamps. By using a special chemical **solvent**, they have been able to successfully extract the rare earth metals from the lamps, remove poisonous mercury from them, and reuse them in color television screens and lamps.

Circuit boards for electronic devices contain valuable rare earth metals that should be recycled.

ENGINEERS OF ALL KINDS

Mechanical and electrical engineers design recycling machines and equipment. They constantly find ways to improve these machines to make them more effective by consuming less energy and fewer raw materials.

One thing they are currently focusing on is finding more ways to automate the recycling process. With fewer workers sorting and dealing with recyclables, the process is faster and safer.

Civil engineers help design buildings that make the best use of resources and energy. Environmental engineers work on new ways to manage and reduce industrial waste produced by MRFs or manufacturers that use recycled materials. They also investigate companies that are accused of violating environmental regulations. They work with the company and government officials to achieve a positive outcome. If actions are needed to correct the problem, the engineers assist or oversee these efforts.

Many new buildings are constructed using recycled materials, such as the metal roof on this building.

Foam products may be convenient and cheap, but they clog our landfills.

PRODUCT DESIGNERS

New recyclable products and products made from recycled materials are constantly arriving in stores. Product designers are in charge of creating and testing these products. They also come up with new ways to recycle, sometimes finding ways to recycle products that have in the past been unrecyclable.

For many years, Styrofoam was not recyclable. Yet this light plastic substance is used worldwide to make plates, coffee cups, packing material, and other products. Styrofoam is not biodegradable. It also contains a chemical called benzene that can cause cancer. However, product designers have recently found a way to shred Styrofoam safely and melt it down under high heat. Then it can be remolded safely into other products. This could help cut down on the amount of Styrofoam that ends up in landfills.

Sherill Baldwin is an environmental analyst with Connecticut's Department of Energy and Environmental Protection. She works on construction and demolition debris recycling, product stewardship, and reuse projects. She has 30 years of experience working in waste management.

When did you first realize you wanted to work in the recycling industry? I grew up in Harwich, Massachusetts, on Cape Cod, where my mother was a naturalist. When I was a child, my mother would walk the wetlands with my brothers and me, and we'd pick up buried objects, tiny treasures such as broken dishes and old medicine bottles. I didn't realize it at the time, but the wetlands my mother was working to preserve were on the site of an old dump. That was my introduction to how we throw away stuff that is valuable.

What did you study in college to prepare you for a career in the recycling industry? I wanted to learn more about waste management and recycling after living in California for a couple of years after high school. I came back to Massachusetts and entered UMass at Amherst in 1989. At the time, they had no major in solid waste management and recycling wasn't widely seen as a career. I had to create my own degree, putting together classes in engineering, business, planning, environmental science, organic agriculture, and policy.

What did you learn in other jobs you held in school that helped you in your career? I went to UMass because I heard they had a recycling club. I soon found out that it had been inactive for five years! So I started up the club again. Soon the university hired me to develop a recycling program for student dormitories and off-campus housing. After graduation, I went to work for the Center for EcoTechnology in Pittsfield, Massachusetts, where the focus was on composting or organics recycling. Then I entered the University of Michigan to earn a degree in resource development. I came back to New England and had several interesting jobs. For a while, I was the ecology director at a spiritual retreat center in Madison, Connecticut. I've been working for the state of Connecticut for seven years.

What project have you worked on that you're especially proud of? The deconstruction industry. It involves dismantling homes and reusing the building materials instead of demolishing them and tossing them into a landfill. The materials that are recovered are sold at building material reuse centers so homeowners and contractors can purchase the used doors, windows, appliances, and flooring for reuse. We have nine reuse centers in Connecticut and hope to see more of them in the future.

It takes a team of people to produce a good recycling program. Does working as part of a team come naturally to you, and how do you handle the other team members when you're the boss? I love collaboration. You learn a lot more that way. When diverse people come together, they have different ideas. Dialogues help get them to the nugget, the concept where all can agree. From there, the group can move forward.

What would your dream project be if you were given unlimited resources? I volunteer for a creative reuse center for the arts, which sells low-cost art supplies to teachers, artists, and the public. The materials are scrap and surplus from industry and businesses. If I could, I would work more with folks who make art or interesting products from scrap.

What advice would you give to young people who want to work in the field of recycling? I would tell them to study a range of subjects in school, because waste management involves everything. Garbage is very personal. You are, in a real sense, what you throw away. When you look into your trash can, you learn a lot about yourself. ✳

MRF employees keep watch over automated sorting machines to make sure they are functioning correctly.

PICKING UP AND PICKING OUT

Many skilled workers are needed to get recyclables to MRFs and process them. Drivers operate recycling trucks as other workers empty the recycling bins into the vehicle. Route managers plot out the truck routes, plan schedules for pickup, and record statistics and data.

At the MRF, sorters separate the different recyclables onto conveyor belts. If the facility is automated, workers are still needed to keep an eye on things and pull out any items that could damage the machinery. Mechanics, technicians, and maintenance workers inspect, repair, and maintain all equipment, including the recycling trucks. Mechanics may be called on to make emergency roadside repairs if a truck breaks down along its route.

MANAGING AND SELLING

MRF managers ensure that facilities run smoothly and that the flow of recyclables is efficient and profitable. They develop budgets, set long-term goals, and deal with the public and the press. They also are responsible for recruiting, hiring, and training workers. Managers evaluate workers' performance and share their feedback with senior managers. They make sure the workplace is safe and give regular safety briefings to workers.

Some companies specialize in purchasing recyclables so they can process them and sell the recycled materials. Sales representatives, also called account managers, find landfills and other facilities that will sell recyclables. After the recyclables are processed into raw materials, the sales representatives seek out businesses and manufacturers who want to buy them. These representatives need to be persuasive salespeople who can give a convincing presentation to potential clients.

A manager supervises other employees and makes sure the recycling operation is working smoothly.

Erika Iris Simmons reuses old cassette tapes to create portraits of stars such as rock musician Jimi Hendrix.

Reusing old things can be a dirty business. However, some people have found ways to create beautiful things using materials that might seem like nothing more than old junk. For example, many of today's artists and craftspeople are finding creative ways to take e-waste of the 1980s and 1990s and upcycle it into works of art and useful products.

UPSCALING THE PAST

Chicago artist Erika Iris Simmons has found a new use for old audiotapes and videocassettes. She spools out the tape and uses it to create portraits of famous people.

Los Angeles designer Chris McCullough also uses old tapes in his art projects. He makes celebrity portraits out of audiocassette cases arranged like tiles. McCullough says he finds it appropriate because "cassettes represent the first portable music medium you could share and personalize yourself."

Ptolemy Elrington hopes his sculptures will encourage people to think about their own personal impact on the environment.

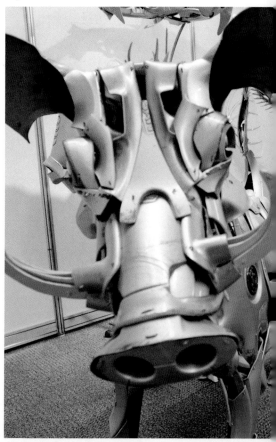

FLOOR LAMPS AND AQUARIUMS

Other artists use large pieces of e-waste to create useful items. Jeff Faber of Oshkosh, Wisconsin, turns old video game consoles such as the Nintendo 64 into lamps. Jake Harris of Hildreth, Nebraska, transforms old computers into aquariums. Other artists convert computer towers into mailboxes and outdoor benches, or computer circuit boards into wall and desk clocks.

Yuken Teruya poses with a tree he sculpted from paper shopping bags.

JUNKYARD SCULPTURES

Some artists transform trash into works of fine art. Michelle Reader of London, England, upcycles materials such as the internal parts of mechanical toys and clocks into sculptures. "I love the unpredictability of found materials and enjoy the invention necessary to transfer them into a sculpture," she says.

Ptolemy Elrington's favorite medium is old car hubcaps. He bends, shapes, and fuses them together to make a shiny fish or a fierce wild boar with pointy tusks.

Yuken Teruya prefers to work with paper products. His *Corner Forest* is composed of tree branches cut from toilet paper rolls and mounted on a wall. His *Constellation* is made up of dark skies of stars fashioned inside paper shopping bags. ☀

SPECIALISTS AND RESEARCHERS

Many people need to be convinced to recycle. They might not be aware of how important and easy it is. Recycling specialists are the public face of recycling. They are employed by environmental service organizations or government agencies. They attend events where recycling and preserving the environment are the focus. They speak to community groups, schools, homeowners' associations, and other organizations to emphasize the importance of recycling programs. They also help prepare educational materials for distribution.

Recycling researchers conduct research on recycled products. They collect data on market demand for products as well as the time and cost required to recycle different items. This information helps them develop plans to improve the recycling facilities that employ them.

Recycling specialists might hold meetings to discuss the best ways of informing people about recycling programs.

Drivers need to get special licenses before they are allowed to operate large vehicles such as recycling trucks.

EDUCATION AND TRAINING

The education requirements for jobs in the recycling and reuse industry vary widely. Scientists and engineers need at least a bachelor's degree. Many of them also have more advanced degrees, and they must continually learn new things throughout their careers to stay in touch with the field's latest developments.

Mechanics and technicians should have at least a high school diploma and a year of on-the-job experience repairing and operating machinery. MRF managers need a bachelor's degree. Many also have a master's degree in business administration or industrial engineering.

Route managers may be hired with a high school education, but would benefit by having several years of experience in waste management or transportation. Drivers need to be high school graduates and should have a commercial driver's license. No specific educational requirements are generally needed for haulers and sorters. However, these workers need to be strong enough to lift heavy bins and items off a conveyor belt.

Recyclables have a long journey to become new products after they are tossed in bins.

4

FROM CURBSIDE TO STORE SHELF

The journey of a recyclable from the consumer who first uses it to the store shelf as a new product is long and eventful. Three important things must happen in any recycling process. The recyclables must first be collected. Then they are treated and processed, sold to manufacturers, and made into new products. Finally, they are put back in circulation. Let's follow the path from your home to the store and see just how recycling works.

HIGHLIGHTS IN RECYCLING TECHNOLOGY

1894	1905	Early 1970s	Late 1990s
One of the first returnable deposit glass bottles is manufactured by the Biedenharn Candy Company of Vicksburg, Mississippi.	New York City burns garbage to generate enough electricity to light the Williamsburg Bridge.	The first recycling trailers pulled behind a garbage truck appear in American towns and cities.	The first single-stream recycling facilities begin operating.

COLLECTING AND DEPOSITING

It's Friday morning, time to put the garbage out for pickup. Along with your trash can, you also carry a bin of recyclables down to the curb. In your neighborhood, recyclables are collected every other week. Your transfer station accepts single streaming, so your bin contains paper, plastic, metal, and glass.

As you set down the bin, you notice the bottle of fruit juice for which you paid an added nickel deposit. You'd like to get that nickel back. So you remove it from the bin and take it down to your local supermarket, along with some other deposit bottles and cans you had set aside earlier. The market has its own recycling center with machines that accept glass and plastic bottles and aluminum cans. You slip a bottle into the slot in the machine and hear it drop and break inside. When you've finished recycling all your bottles, you press a button and the machine gives you a receipt for the total amount of your deposits. You can spend the amount on the receipt as credit in the market.

Taking your recycling bins to the curb or your local recycling center is just the first step in the recycling process.

Trucks unload materials into piles at a recycling center in New York City.

TO THE TRANSFER STATION

The shredded plastic, broken glass, and crushed cans from the store recycling machines will be removed once the machine is full. These materials are then collected and delivered to a manufacturer to be made into new products.

The bins the recycling truck picks up at your curbside have a longer journey. They are first brought to your town's transfer station and unloaded from the trucks into large dumpsters. Once they are full, the dumpsters are loaded onto flatbed trucks and delivered to an MRF. There the recyclables will be sorted and bundled.

WHERE THE MAGIC HAPPENS

A Recology employee sorts materials at an MRF in San Francisco.

RECOLOGY

Among the U.S. cities most committed to recycling is San Francisco, California. San Francisco's success in reducing waste is due in large part to Recology. This waste mangagement company, owned and operated by its employees, is on the cutting edge of recycling. With Recology's help, San Francisco has reduced its discarded waste from 900,000 tons in 2000 to nearly half that by 2009. By 2020, the city hopes to become America's first zero-waste community.

THREE BINS

Recology has given every city household three bins to fill. The blue bin is for all accepted recyclable products. The green

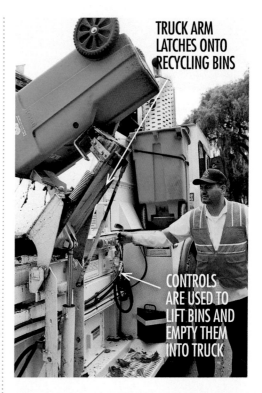

TRUCK ARM LATCHES ONTO RECYCLING BINS

CONTROLS ARE USED TO LIFT BINS AND EMPTY THEM INTO TRUCK

Color-coded bins make it easy for people to separate recyclables, compostables, and trash.

bin is for food scraps, plant material, and paper that has been soiled by food. The black bin is for trash that doesn't fit into those categories.

People in San Francisco are required to participate in this program. Those who don't put out their bins or separate recyclables properly are given a warning, If they still don't follow the rules after receiving a warning, a fine is imposed. To educate the public on this program, Recology sends representatives to meet with residents and provides a lively online video that explains recycling.

ADVISE AND CONSULT

Recology sells its compost materials to area farms and vineyards to be used as fertilizer for soil. For a fee, reps will advise farmers on how to best use the compost to benefit crops. Recology is considering creating a consulting division to handle the many inquiries from visiting officials who want to

learn how to bring better recycling methods to their own cities and countries. The company's goal is to retire every landfill in California and eventually the entire nation. "To me, that's not waste management," Recology president and CEO Michael J. Sangiacomo says of landfills. "It's just putting waste in a hole in the ground and hoping nothing goes wrong. If you can put waste back into commerce, that's much smarter. ✳

Composting produces a rich, soil-like material that helps plants grow.

A worker inspects bales of recycled plastic.

ON TO THE MRF

At the MRF, recyclables travel along conveyor belts where the sorting begins. First, cardboard boxes and plastic bags are removed from the stream so they won't jam the automated sorting machines. Heavier metals and glass products are separated from lighter plastics and paper. The paper stream is separated into newspapers, glossy magazine paper, computer paper, and scrap paper. Magnets are used to separate metals containing iron, such as tin and steel cans, from those that do not contain iron, such as aluminum cans. The magnets attract the iron objects and repel the non-iron ones. Both will be recycled. Glass is separated by color—clear, amber, green, and brown. Once sorted, each kind of recyclable is ready to be bundled or baled. Then it is sold and shipped to manufacturers that will break the recyclables down into their raw materials to make new products.

FROM PAPER TO PULP

Papermaking companies shred recycled paper and place it in machines called pulpers along with water and chemicals. The liquid is heated to quickly break down the paper into fibers. The result is a soupy pulp. The pulp is forced through screens that remove such contaminants as glue and plastic. Next it enters rapidly spinning cone-shaped cylinders. Heavy contaminants such as staples and paper clips fly out of the cone, while smaller ones are collected in the center and later removed. Water is used to rinse any remaining ink from the pulp.

The pulp is beaten to further break down the fibers into smaller pieces. Any dye is then stripped from color paper using chemicals. This turns the pulp brown. If white paper is desired, the pulp is bleached using more chemicals. This pulp can be used to make new paper.

A worker shows off paper pulp at a factory in the Netherlands.

SHREDDED PAPER IS MIXED WITH WATER IN LARGE VATS

LASTING CONTRIBUTION

You have probably used one of Craig Busch's classic blue recycling bins.

THE BLUE BIN

Recycling technology has advanced in many ways since the early 1980s. However, one thing has not changed—the bright blue recycling bins left curbside in towns and cities across North America. The blue bin was the invention of Craig Busch, a Canadian college student. Curbside pickup was a new program in Canada at the time. Busch came up with a lightweight, durable bin that people

could fill with recyclables. In 1981, the blue bins were used for the first time in test neighborhoods in Kitchener, Ontario.

A CURBSIDE EXPERIMENT

The Kitchener government experimented with several different methods of curbside pickup. In one, the blue bins were used. In another, no blue bins were provided. The blue bin proved the most popular option among the townspeople. Two years later,

Recycling containers of all kinds are colored blue today because of Craig Busch's original design.

Blue recycling bins usually display the universal recycling logo.

the entire town was provided with blue bins. In 1985, Busch and a partner started Busch Systems to manufacture recycling bins on a large scale. Soon the blue bins were appearing across Canada and the United States.

WHY BLUE?

Busch picked the color blue not only because it looked nice but also because it would be easy for truck drivers to see. Blue also proved best in withstanding damage and fading from exposure to the Sun's **ultraviolet** light as bins sat at

the curb. Originally the blue bins were manufactured in only one size. Because recycling has grown more popular, they are now available in many different sizes to accommodate people's different needs. Many state and local governments provide residents with one free bin, with the option to purchase more if needed. Along with the blue color, the bins still display the universal recycling logo and the proud words "WE RECYCLE." ✳

GLASS AND METAL MADE ANEW

At a glassmaking plant, crushed glass is ground down into cullet. All contaminants must be removed from the cullet before it can be processed. A magnetic field removes metal bottle caps. Any bits of plastic or paper are removed by hand or machine. Fine screens filter out any ceramic bits. At this point, the cleaned cullet is melted down and decolorized with chemicals. If a new color is needed, the cullet is dyed. The cullet is sold to manufacturers who melt it and place it into molds, letting it harden into new jars, bottles, and other objects. When these are discarded, the recycling process is repeated. Glass can be recycled forever. This is a very good feature, since glass bottles will never decompose in a landfill.

At a processing plant, aluminum cans are melted down. Then the molten aluminum is hardened into giant blocks called ingots. Each ingot is composed of about 1.6 million beverage cans. The ingots go to mills. There, they are rolled out into thin layers and used to make new products. Aluminum can be recycled faster than any other material. The entire process can take less than 60 days.

A worker inspects aluminum ingots at a warehouse.

Plastic pellets can be molded into new plastic products.

PLASTICS TRANSFORMED

Plastic bottles and containers are put through a machine where sharp blades chip or shred them into tiny pieces. Plastic bags are also cut apart. However, they are chopped up using large blades. The bits of plastic are washed in a strong solution of water and detergents to remove all liquid residue and paper labels. The pieces are then melted down and put through a machine called an extruder. The extruder molds the melted plastic into thin tubes that resemble noodles. Spinning knives cut the tubes into small pellets. The pellets can be molded into new plastic products. Some become bottles again. Others become such diverse products as kitchenware, countertops, and outdoor furniture.

Many items proudly advertise that they are made from recycled materials.

BACK ON THE SHELF

Once the products are finished, they are sold and shipped out to stores across the country. Manufacturers mark recycled products, especially paper and plastic items, with symbols and codes that inform shoppers they are made from recyclables. Look for these items at stores. When you buy a recycled product, you are helping the environment and giving your support to the recycling industry. You are also sending a message to manufacturers that they should create more goods using recycled materials. The next time you buy a bottle of fruit juice, think about the recycled glass that made it. And don't forget to return it for your deposit!

SUMMING UP

Recycling is off to a good start. But we still have a long way to go. Too many people continue to toss bottles, cans, and other recyclables into their garbage cans, and these items end up clogging landfills. Other trash ends up in waterways, polluting them and killing fish and plants. Garbage burned in incinerators sends toxins into the air we breathe. Garbage pollutes our entire environment.

In addition, precious energy and resources are expended making new products instead of reusing or recycling old ones. While recycling should be a global effort, it has to start with individuals. How can you do a better job of reusing the resources in your life? Or even better, maybe you'd like to help out by getting a job in the recycling industry one day. If each of us pitches in and recycles, a society with zero waste may become a reality.

ANA MARTINEZ DE LUCO

In the Williamsburg area of Brooklyn, New York, is a huge can-and-bottle redemption center called Sure We Can. It is operated by Sister Ana Martinez de Luco, who sees her mission as both saving the environment and saving people. Every day, needy people bring shopping carts to the center filled with discarded cans and bottles they have gathered. They exchange these recyclables for money. On an average summer day, Martinez de Luco redeems 40,000 cans and bottles. The "canners," as they are called, also help her collect and sort the bottles and cans.

Pollution, a major problem everywhere, could be substantially reduced by a worldwide commitment to recycling.

THE FUTURE

Plasma arc recycling uses high heat to turn discarded products into energy.

PLASMA ARC RECYCLING

While turning recyclable products into new products is important, scientists have discovered that many discarded products, including nonrecyclable ones, can be turned into energy. Plasma arc recycling heats solid waste at extremely high temperatures. This produces a gas that can be burned for energy as well as a hard, rocklike substance that can be made into a building material. Because the temperatures are so high, most of the toxic chemicals in the products are burned away.

Plasma arc recycling is fairly rare today. The process is still controversial. Some critics claim that despite precautions, it still releases harmful chemicals into the atmosphere. The most successful plasma arc recycling plant opened in England in 2007.

A WATER-RECYCLING SHOWER

New inventions are improving recycling. One of the most interesting is a water-recycling shower created by several inventors in Britain and Sweden over the past several years. Daily showering is one of the greatest wastes of fresh water in many countries. This innovative shower cleans, filters, and recycles 70 percent of the water it uses. In an average four-person household, it could save 20,000 to 40,000 gallons (75,708 to 151,416 liters) of water every year.

RECYCLING APPS

Encouraging more people to recycle is a top priority. Participants in the 2014 Recycling Challenge came up with some original Web apps that could motivate people to recycle. One proposed app, called CycleUp, would give each resident of a community a ranking based on how much he or she recycles. It would rate everybody against their neighbors, to spark friendly competition. The app would also encourage entire neighborhoods to compete against one another within their city for first place in recycling. Another app would tell users how to recycle a product when they scan its bar code into their phone. They would also receive information about why this product should be recycled.

Some water recycling systems use the water from sinks and showers to keep lawns and gardens green.

CAREER STATS

ENVIRONMENTAL SCIENTISTS

MEDIAN ANNUAL SALARY (2012): $63,570

NUMBER OF JOBS (2012): 90,000

PROJECTED JOB GROWTH (2012–2022): 15%, faster than average

PROJECTED INCREASE IN JOBS (2012–2022): 13,200

REQUIRED EDUCATION: Bachelor's degree

LICENSE/CERTIFICATION: None

ENVIRONMENTAL ENGINEERING TECHNICIANS

MEDIAN ANNUAL SALARY (2012): $43,350

NUMBER OF JOBS (2012): 19,000

PROJECTED JOB GROWTH (2012–2022): 18%, faster than average

PROJECTED INCREASE IN JOBS (2012–2022): 3,500

REQUIRED EDUCATION: Associate's degree

LICENSE/CERTIFICATION: None

MRF HANDLERS AND SORTERS

MEDIAN ANNUAL SALARY (2012): $22,970

NUMBER OF JOBS (2012): 3,428,800

PROJECTED JOB GROWTH (2012–2022): 10%, as fast as average

PROJECTED INCREASE IN JOBS (2012–2022): 341,700

REQUIRED EDUCATION: Less than high school

LICENSE/CERTIFICATION: None

Figures reported by the United States Bureau of Labor Statistics

RESOURCES

BOOKS

Green, Robert. *From Waste to Energy*. Ann Arbor, MI: Cherry Lake Publishing, 2013.

Mooney, Carla. *Recycling*. Chicago: Norwood House Press, 2014.

Palmer, Erin. *Recycling, Yes or No*. Vero Beach, FL: Rourke Educational Media, 2015.

FACTS FOR NOW

Visit this Scholastic Web site for more information
on recycling and upcycling:
www.factsfornow.scholastic.com
Enter the keywords **Recycling and Upcycling**

GLOSSARY

alloys (AL-oiz) metals made from mixing other metals, or mixing a metal with an element that is not a metal

biodegrade (bye-oh-di-GRAYD) break down by natural processes

compost (KAHM-post) a mixture of organic material, such as rotted leaves, vegetables, or manure, that is added to soil to make it more productive

conservation (kahn-sur-VAY-shuhn) the protection of valuable things, especially forests, wildlife, natural resources, or artistic or historic objects

contaminated (kuhn-TAM-i-nay-tid) containing harmful or undesirable substances

dumps (DUHMPS) areas of land where people deposit garbage without any environmental protection, compaction, or plan for completion

epidemics (ep-i-DEM-iks) infectious diseases present in a large number of people at the same time

fluoresce (fluh-RESS) to release radiation in the form of visible light

municipal (myoo-NISS-uh-puhl) relating to a town or city or its local government

pulp (PUHLP) any soft, wet mixture

rationed (RASH-uhnd) gave out resources in limited amounts

sanitation (san-i-TAY-shuhn) systems for cleaning the water supply and disposing of sewage and garbage in a town or city

solvent (SAHL-vuhnt) a substance, usually a liquid, that can make another substance dissolve

transfer station (TRANS-fur STAY-shuhn) a holding area from which trash is taken to a landfill or a Materials Recovery Facility

ultraviolet (uhl-truh-VYE-uh-lit) a type of light that cannot be seen by the human eye

upcycle (UHP-sye-kuhl) to put a discarded product to a new use

INDEX

Page numbers in *italics* indicate illustrations.

INDEX *(CONTINUED)*

ABOUT THE AUTHOR

STEVEN OTFINOSKI has written more than 175 books for young readers, including books on forensics, computers, and rockets. He fills his recycling bins every week and uses cloth bags at the supermarket. He lives in Connecticut.